PC Selby

SIMON AND SCHUSTER

PC Selby and Lucy
Police House
Garner Bridge
Greendale

Come and say hello to PC Selby!

PC Selby is the local policeman, on hand to keep the peace and sort out tricky traffic jams. There's not much crime in Greendale, but he never knows when his detective skills might be needed...

As usual, PC Selby was up and out on the beat straight after breakfast.

"Morning!" he said, as he pedalled past Pat's house.

"Hello Arthur," answered Pat. "What a beautiful day! Sara's going to spend it in the garden."

Sara nodded and smiled, then stopped in her tracks. "I don't believe it."

"It's my geraniums — they've moved!" Sara said.

PC Selby climbed off his bike. "Where's me notebook?"

"I planted the red ones over here," she explained, pointing at the flowerbeds. "And the pink ones over there."

"Are you sure?" said Pat.

"She's right Dad," Julian piped up, "they've swapped places."

"I better look into this at once," said PC Selby.

Before the policeman could get home to review the evidence, Ajay flagged him down.

"Something's happened on the platform," he cried, "to the hanging baskets."

"What appears to be the problem?" PC Selby asked.

"All the pansies have gone, disappeared!"

PC Selby scratched his head. What was going on?

When Pat delivered his afternoon post, PC Selby still hadn't solved the mystery.

"Plants don't move about by themselves," he frowned.

"It's almost as if there's a Phantom Gardener on the loose," agreed Pat.

"Exactly!" said PC Selby. "I'll start questioning the villagers at once."

First stop was Dr Gilbertson's surgery.

"Dorothy Thompson told me that her roses have been pruned," said Dr Gilbertson. "But she hasn't touched them in weeks."

PC Selby sipped his tea. "So the Phantom Gardener strikes again."

"Sorry?"

"Oh er, nothing!" he replied. "Carry on."

"This morning I found that my patio pots had been replanted... with pansies!"

Every night PC Selby paced round his front room, trying to solve the puzzle.

"Maybe it's a stray dog looking for a bone," he pondered.

"Dogs can't trim roses or plant flowers!" said Lucy. "If you want to catch the Phantom Gardener, you'll have to sit up and wait for them."

"A stakeout!" PC Selby cried with excitement. "I'll phone Pat for back-up."

The next night, PC Selby, Pat and Jess sat down to wait in Greendale Post Office.

"We can see the whole High Street from here," said Pat.

"Just the place," agreed PC Selby.

Everybody got comfy. So comfy, that Pat and Jess started to fall asleep.

PC Selby was nodding off too, when – snap!

There was someone outside!

PC Selby nudged Pat, then grabbed his torch.
He crept outside and switched it on.

"Stop in the name of the law!" he cried.
"I've caught you red-handed."

The light shone on a figure carrying a trowel.
It slowly turned round.

Pat and PC Selby both shouted at once.
"Reverend Timms!"

Reverend Timms was very confused. "Must water my prize blooms..."

"You've been sleepwalking," said Pat. "Come in and have some cocoa."

As the Reverend woke up, PC Selby explained what had happened.

"Heavens above!" he said. "To think I'm the Phantom Gardener."

"No harm done," PC Selby replied. "At least the case is now closed."

"All thanks to our trusty village policeman!" said Pat.

SIMON AND SCHUSTER

First published in 2005 in Great Britain by Simon & Schuster UK Ltd
Africa House, 64-78 Kingsway, London WC2B 6AH

Postman Pat® © 2005 Woodland Animations, a division of Entertainment Rights PLC
Licensed by Entertainment Rights PLC
Original television design by Ivor Wood
From the original writer John Cunliffe

Royal Mail and Post Office imagery is used by kind permission of Royal Mail Group plc
All rights reserved

Text by Mandy Archer © 2005 Simon & Schuster UK Ltd
Illustrations by Baz Rowell © 2005 Simon & Schuster UK Ltd

A CIP catalogue record for this book is available from the British Library upon request

ISBN 1416901825
Printed in China

1 3 5 7 9 10 8 6 4 2